A Gift For:

_____

From:

_____

Copyright © 2014 Hallmark Licensing, LLC

Published by Hallmark Gift Books,
a division of Hallmark Cards, Inc.,
Kansas City, MO 64141
Visit us on the Web at Hallmark.com.

Editorial Director: Carrie Bolin
Editor: Emily Osborn
Art Director: Jan Mastin
Designer: Bryan Ring
Production Artist: Bryan Ring

ISBN:978-1-59530-894-8
EWM3079

Printed and bound in China
NOV13

J.B. and the Dance Contest

by **Molly Wigand** Illustrated by **Lynda Calvert-Weyant**

Hallmark

Introducing J.B. Bunny
(J.B. stands for "Jelly Bean!").
He's the hippest hoppest dude
that anybunny's ever seen!

This hare can bust a move,
and believe me, he's not shy!
Yep, no one dances wilder
than this crazy bouncin' guy!

After years of entertaining friends
with all his jammin' grooves,
he decided to "go pro"
and show the world his righteous moves!

He became a dance contestant
for Big Bunny's Talent Hour.
He stood before the judges
and unleashed his boppin' power!

See, J.B. had a secret
that enhanced his winning chances—
the jelly beans he ate
made him do some crazy dances!

He started with a GREEN one.
Then his cottontail got wiggly—
it started twitching back and forth
and made his paws all jiggly!

"That bunny dude can twist!"
said the judges to the crowd.
They gave him perfect 10s—
then the cheering got real loud!

J.B. tried another bean—
this time he switched to YELLOW!
He changed into a fancy tux—
and became a waltzing fellow!

Up on his toes he whirled and twirled, counting 1, 2, 3 . . .
Around the floor he glided
just as graceful as can be!

Again, the judges marveled
at his pure finesse and grace,
the other dancers did their thing—
but J.B. set the pace!

RED jelly beans came next,
and J.B. stretched his disco muscle.
He struck a funky pose
and then began to do the Hustle!

The crowd adored this bunny;
you could tell from all the cheers.
And it wasn't just his paws that danced—
he even moved his ears!

J.B. was on a roll now,
and the next bean up was PINK—
the band brought in a tuba
and our hero was in sync!

"The Easter Bunny Polka, please?"
was J.B.'s next request—
he polka-ed like a maniac.
This bunny was the best!

By now the other bunnies
were feeling quite left out—
it didn't seem quite fair!
J.B. would win without a doubt!

They asked the judges nicely
if the dance contest was done—
"Just standing here and watching
really isn't that much fun!"

J.B. overheard them
and he thought for just a minute—
"You're right!" he said. "This dance-off
needs a bunch more bunnies in it!

"Just follow what I'm doing,
and then we can all be winners.
Come on! There's room for everyone!
Even you beginners!"

As the bunnies jumped to join him,
J.B. ate a PURPLE bean.
Then he helped every bunny
be a salsa dance machine!

"Try orange!" the bunnies said,
and J.B. gobbled that bean down—
and they started Macarena-ing
like crazy through the town!

"I've got a wild idea,
when we start to dance again,
I'm going to try a bunch of beans
and see what happens then!"

Within a couple seconds,
all those beans began to work—
all at once, he did the hula, tango,
and the jerk!

The bunnies danced that crazy dance
'til they could dance no more,
and then they all collapsed in giggles
right there upon the floor.

Was J.B. glad he shared the spotlight?
Yes, he was! You bet!
This was the kind of Easter
that no-bunny could forget!

**If you have enjoyed this book
or it has touched your life in some way,
we would love to hear from you.**

Please send your comments to:
Hallmark Book Feedback
P.O. Box 419034
Mail Drop 100
Kansas City, MO 64141

Or e-mail us at:
booknotes@hallmark.com